WITCHES'
Night Before
HALLOWEEN

WITCHES' Night Before HALLOWEEN

By Lesley Pratt Bannatyne
Illustrated by Adrian Tans

PELICAN PUBLISHING COMPANY
GRETNA 2007

For Evan and Maya and, of course, Maggie—L. P. B.

For my mother—A. T.

*The word "Pelican" and the depiction of a pelican are trademarks
of Pelican Publishing Company, Inc., and are registered in the
U.S. Patent and Trademark Office.*

Library of Congress Cataloging-in-Publication Data

Bannatyne, Lesley Pratt.
  Witches' night before Halloween / Lesley Pratt Bannatyne ;
illustrated by Adrian Tans.
    p. cm.
  ISBN 978-1-58980-485-2 (hardcover : alk. paper)
  1. Halloween—Juvenile poetry. 2. Children's poetry, American. I.
Title.
  PS3602.A666W58 2007
  811'.6—dc22

                                        2007008472

Printed in Singapore
Published by Pelican Publishing Company, Inc.
1000 Burmaster Street, Gretna, Louisiana 70053

**Witches' Night
Before Halloween**

'Twas the night before Halloween and all through the cottages, The witches were stirring their brews and their potages.

Their cupboards were bursting with
  hoptoads and newts,
And they'd shined up their pointy-
  toed, fancy-dress boots.

The witchlings lay snoring, quite snug
    in their beds,
With visions of moist, creeping things
    in their heads.

"Nice night," whispered Mad-Maud to Potbelly-Pat
As she snuffed out the torches and took in the cat.

But at the first stroke of midnight, when folks lay asleep,
The whole gang of witches on tiptoes did creep
Out through the cornfields and 'neath the troll's bridge
Past the shadowy crossroads to Cemetery Ridge.

"It's time to begin," hissed Elise-With-One-Eye
As the moon reached its peak in the October sky.

On the stump of a tree, with a thump and a creak,
Big-Bree drummed a beat as the witches all shrieked:
"Come goblins! Come ghosties! Come skeleton bones!
We've witch work tonight! We can't do it alone!"

They stomped on the ground! They bellowed! (They wheezed.)
They tangoed! And salsa-ed! (On arthritic knees.)
Louder and wilder with each passing verse
They chanted in voices from tuneless to worse.

Till—*BANG!*—the old charnel house doors cracked and broke,
And out flew their pals with a big blast of smoke:

A few drooling ghouls from down underneath,
With cleanly picked bones and half-rotten teeth;

A pale, dark-eyed viscount quite long in the tooth;
Two squadrons of zombies unkempt and uncouth;

Dark, furry, four-footed hard-to-see things
That take to the sky amidst flutter of wings;
Red-headed banshees with ear-splitting wails;
And a rheumy-eyed ghost dressed in neatly pressed tails.

With one bony finger, Maud tested the breeze,
Grabbed hold of her broom, and ascended with ease.
"To town!" she commanded. "There's much to be done.
Pack your newts and your spiders. Let's go have some fun!"

They dangled black bats from the city hall eaves
And festooned each doorway with poisonous leaves.

Cobwebs were stretched from church spire to town square,
And green slime was dribbled down every porch stair.

On each hollow pumpkin they scratched a mad grin,
Set the kitty-cats yowling, and stoked up the wind.

"So much haunting to get done in so little time,"
Mourned a vain, headless countess a bit past
  her prime.
"Not to mention the rusty old gates we back-
  ordered
Are stuck in a truck at the Canadian border."

"Not like the old days," whined Snaggle-Tooth-Ruth.
"Is this the example we set for our youth?"

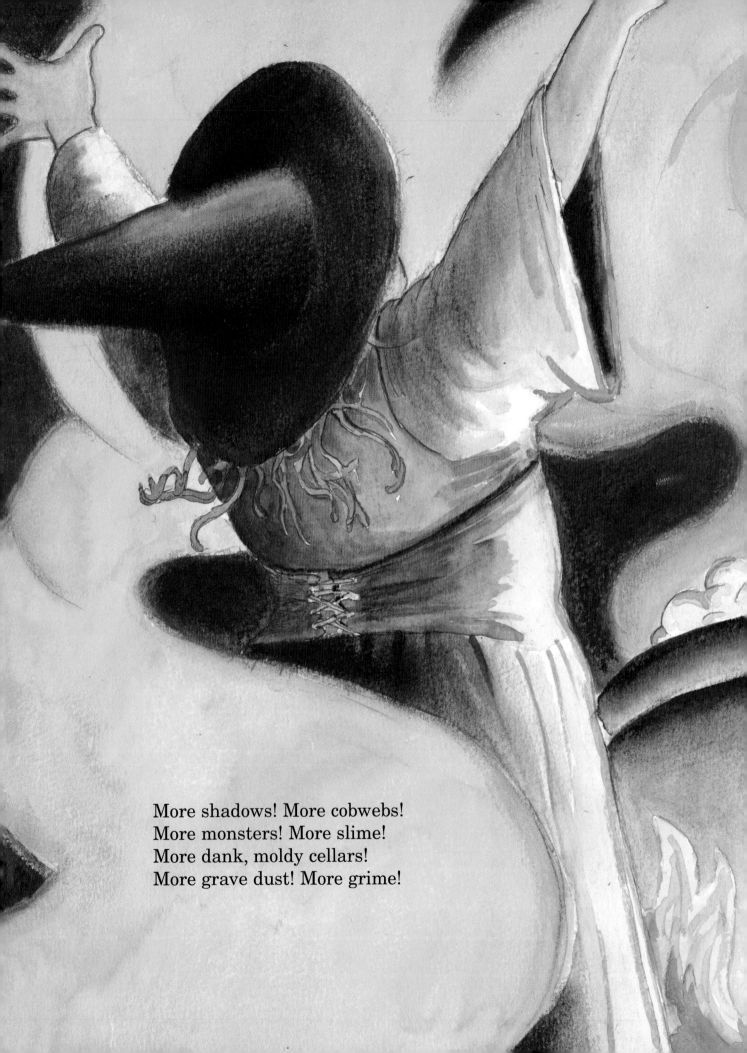

More shadows! More cobwebs!
More monsters! More slime!
More dank, moldy cellars!
More grave dust! More grime!

And when they had finished, thick fog hugged the ground,
So they snapped a few photos and flew out of town.

"To the hovels! Let's go! Time to wake up the spawn!"
Cried the witches while hobbling back home 'cross the lawn.

They banged pots together, poked the witchlings with sticks,
Till the kiddies woke up and threw terrible fits.
"It's Halloween, you gremlins!" crooned Bubonic-Sue.
"Time to show all the humans what witches can do!"

At that the wee witchlings leapt straight from their beds,
Tied pointy black caps to their misshapen heads,
Laced up their brat boots, grabbed onto their brooms,
And rode single file toward the just-risen moon.

"Stay warm! Make good choices!"
cried the parental group,
As the young witches spun some
backflips with a whoop,

And yelled loud as they could while
they sailed through the night:
"Happy Halloween to all
and to all a good fright!"